Santa Claus Is Comin' to Town

ISBN 0-439-82088-X

Copyright © 1934, renewed 1962 by Leo Feist Inc. and Haven Gillespie Music.
All rights for the United States controlled and administered by EMI Feist Catalog Inc.
and Haven Gillespie Music. Rights assigned to EMI Catalogue Partnership. All rights for
the world excluding United States controlled and administered by EMI Feist Catalog Inc.
All rights reserved/International copyright secured/Used by permission. Illustrations
copyright © 2004 by Steven Kellogg. Published by Scholastic Inc., 557 Broadway,
New York, NY 10012, by arrangement with HarperCollins Publishers. SCHOLASTIC
and associated logos are trademarks and/or registered trademarks of Scholastic Inc.

12 11 10 9 8 7 6 5 4 3 2   6 7 8 9 10/0

Printed in the U.S.A.   40

First Scholastic printing, November 2005

Typography by Martha Rago and Amelia Anderson

To Helen, with love

Santa Claus Is Comin' to Town

Written by
J. Fred Coots & Haven Gillespie
illustrated by Steven Kellogg

SCHOLASTIC INC.
New York Toronto London Auckland Sydney
Mexico City New Delhi Hong Kong Buenos Aires

I just came back
from a lovely trip
Along the Milky Way,
I stopped off at the
North Pole
To spend a holiday;

I called on
dear old
Santa Claus
To see what
I could see,

He took me to
his workshop

And told his plans
to me.

OH!

You better watch out,
you better not cry,

Better not pout,
I'm telling you why:

Santa Claus is comin' to town.

He's making a list and checking it twice,

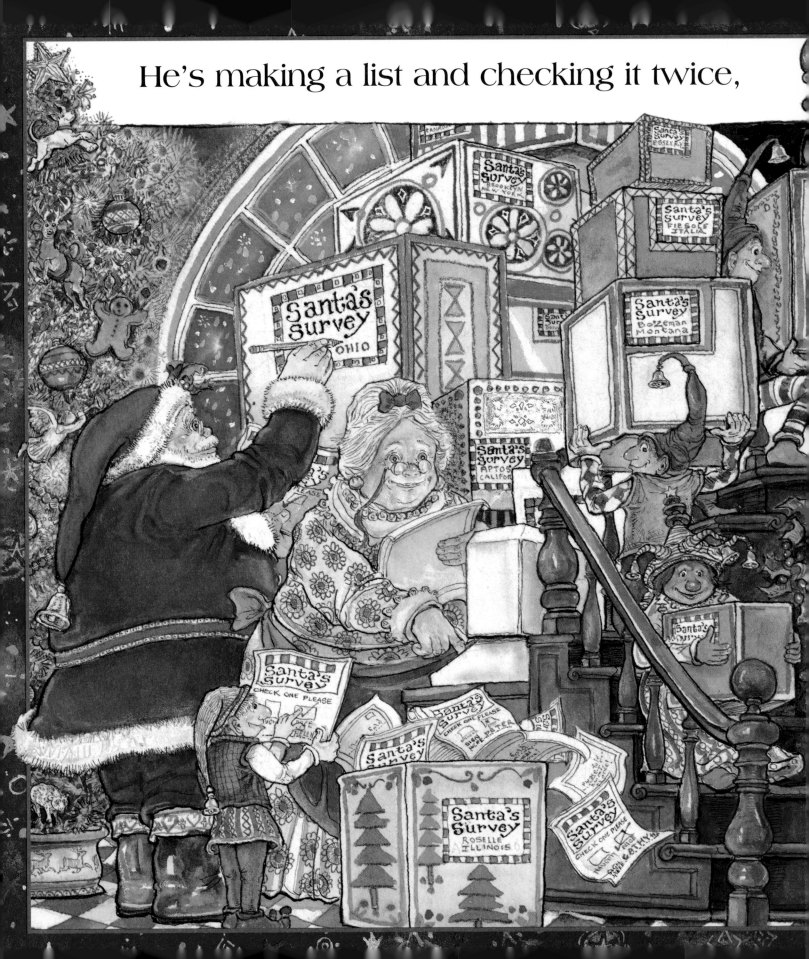

Gonna find out who's naughty and nice,

Santa Claus is comin' to town.

He sees you when you're sleepin',

He knows when you're awake,

He knows if you've been bad

No!

or good,

Please may I help?

So be good for goodness sake.

OH! You better watch out, you better not cry,
Better not pout, I'm telling you why:

Santa
Claus
is
comin'
to
town.

With little tin horns and little toy drums,

Rooty-toot-toots and rummy-tum-tums,

Santa Claus is comin'

TO TOWN

Elephants,

kiddie cars too,

Santa Claus is comin' to TOWN

PLEASE
SLOW DOWN

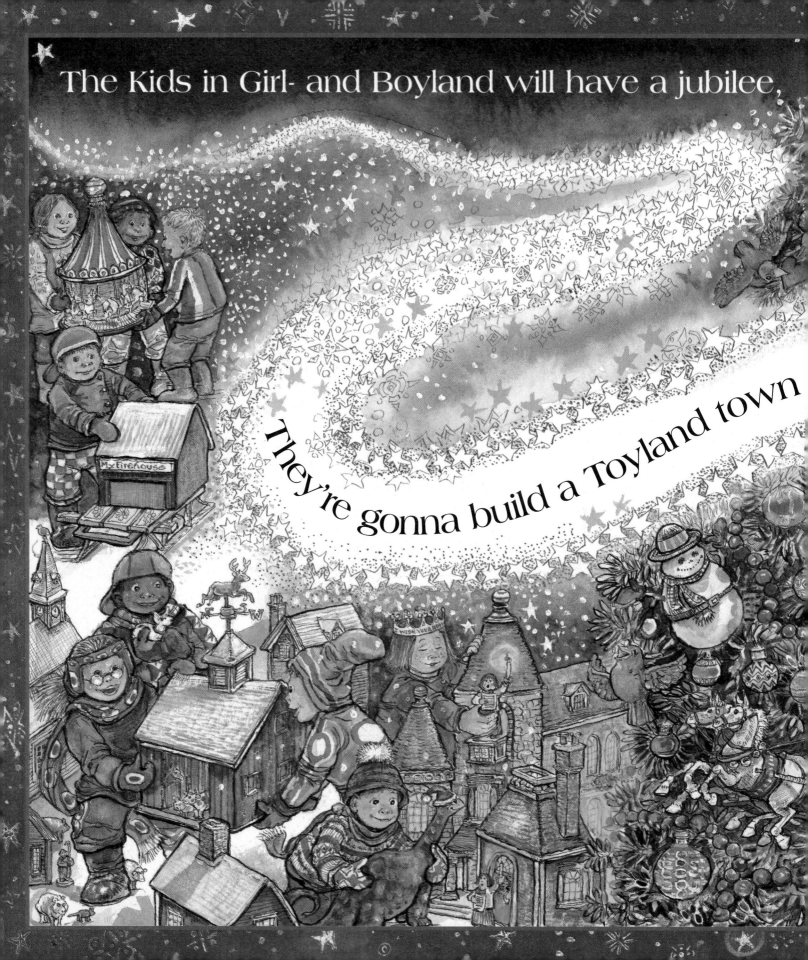

The Kids in Girl- and Boyland will have a jubilee,

They're gonna build a Toyland town

all around the Christmas tree.

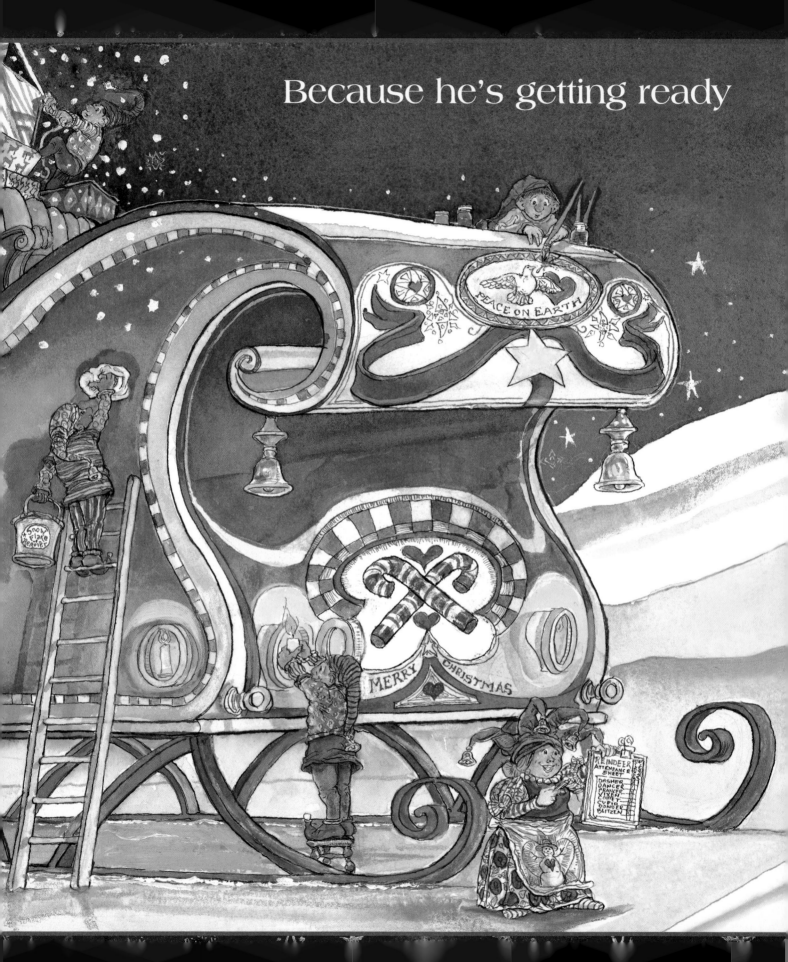

Because he's getting ready

ARCTIC AIRLINES

Now Santa is a busy man,
He has no time to play

You'd better write your letter now

So,

His reindeers and his sleigh.

You better watch out,
you better not cry,
Better not pout,
I'm telling you why:

Santa Claus is comin' to town.